BIG BAD WOLF

BY CLAIRE MASUREL
ILLUSTRATED BY MELISSA IWAI

*To Miss Kini —
Enjoy
Kathy Paul*

SCHOLASTIC INC.
New York Toronto London Auckland Sydney Mexico City
New Delhi Hong Kong Buenos Aires

Cartwheel BOOKS

Deep in the dark, dark forest, there lived a wolf.
People called him BIG BAD WOLF!

Although they had never met him,
people said...

"BIG BAD WOLF
has pointy ears
and shiny eyes!"

He did.

People said…

"BIG BAD WOLF
has a long snout
and sharp teeth!"

He did.

People said . . .

WOLF
y tail
ing howl!"

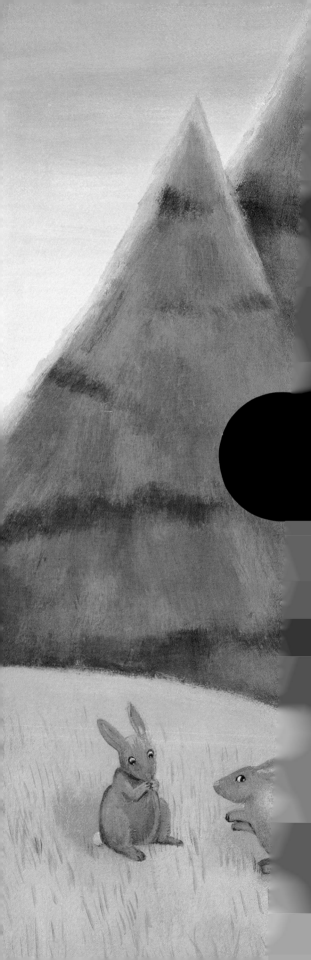